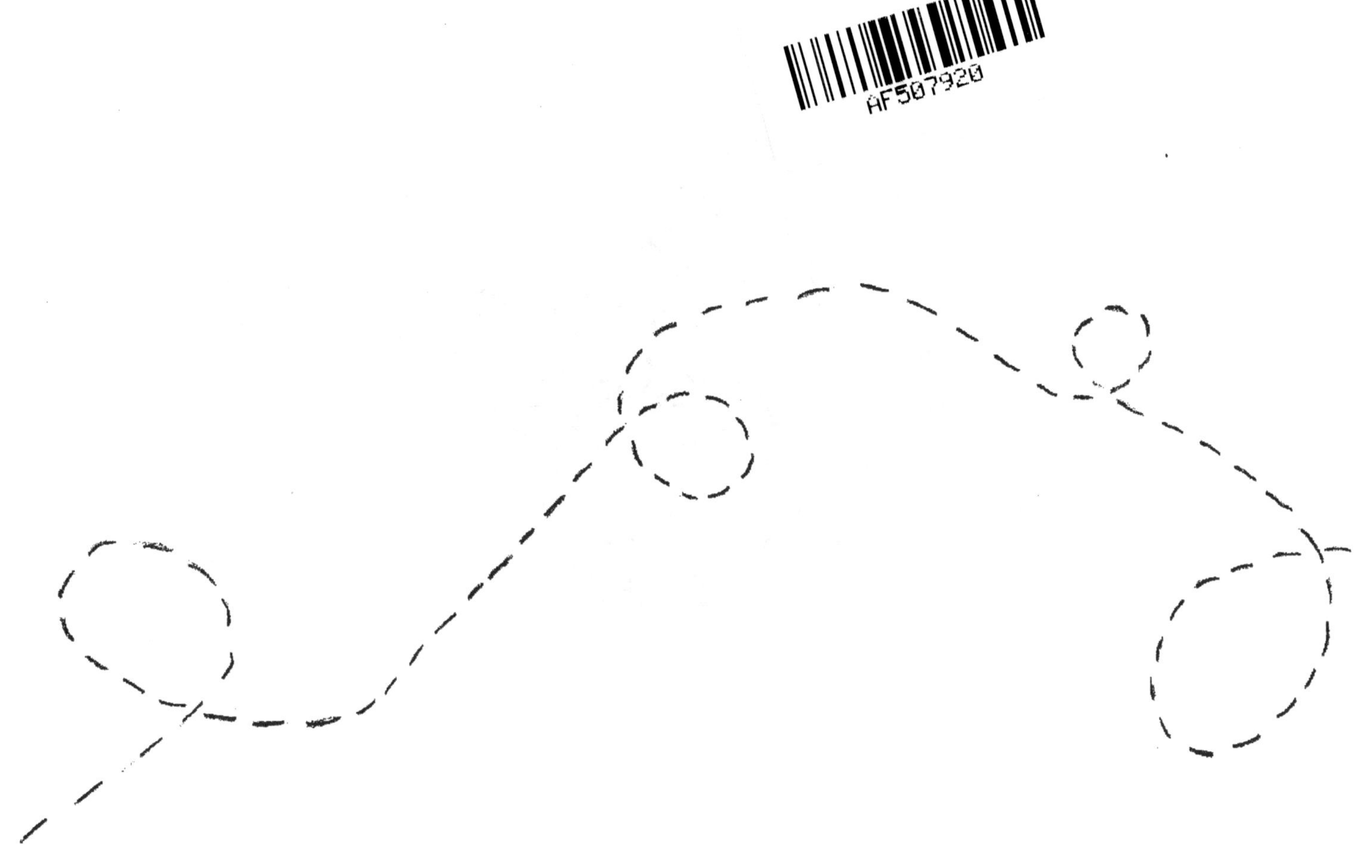

Sophie's Daddy

Written by: Sophie Dolson and Tina Anderson
Illustrated by: Sophie Dolson and Tina Anderson

Illustrations in this book were created from real photographs and thoughtfully transformed into artwork with the assistance of AI.

ISBN: 979-8-9959622-0-5

Library of Congress Control Number: 2026911473

Published by:
The Grands Book Collection

For my son and granddaughter.
I love watching you love her.

My Daddy loves me big

big big

When I want him to wake up

early early early

I climb onto his bed
and say

Daddy Daddy Daddy

Daddy asks if it is **tickle time**
and I say yes yes yes

But
sometimes
I say
no no no

We wash our hands
swish   swish   swish

We wash our faces

splash   splash   splash

We brush our teeth
scrub
scrub
scrub

and pack some snacks

yum

yum

yum

We ride our bike to the park
zoom   zoom   zoom

to swing swing swing

and slide
slide
slide

climb
climb
and climb

and play play play

I run to him fast   fast   fast

And he throws me

high
high
high

When it is time
for bed,
I bring

my

books

tuck tuck tuck
read read read

'Goodnight Sophie,
Daddy loves you
big

big big'

About the Author

Sophie Dolson and Tina Anderson (Grandma) create Sophie's Stories (Series).

Come grow with me!

Check out all the books Grandma is creating with my cousins too.

Aspen and the Magic Ring (Series)
by Aspen Fowler and Tina Anderson

Trouble with Bo (Series)
by Bo Fowler and Tina Anderson

THE GRANDS
BOOK COLLECTION